AF480930

What happened to my tooth?

Julia Johnson

What happened to my tooth?

Julia Johnson

ISBN:
9798830524322

DEDICATION

To my amazing kiddos, Lillian, Scarlett, and Jensen. I hope you never lose your sense of wonder. Also, to my husband for being my rock. Thank you for always encouraging me to follow my dreams.

"Dad look what the tooth fairy gave me!"
"Oh, wow!"
From the Tooth Fairy

"Dad what do you think the tooth fairy did with my tooth?"
"She probably put it in her pocket."

"Or maybe, she has a machine that turns teeth into money. She's probably rich!"
Tooth Fairy Notes
Start
Stop
Speed up
money
Coins
Weight
Size
Density
Clean%
Total Value
Empty Bin
Child's Gift
Property of the Tooth Fairy

"Maybe she just builds a castle with it.
They are nice and strong."

"Or maybe she had to trade the teeth to pirates. The pirates let her enter their mysterious caves to find gold."

"And the pirates use the teeth to build strong weapons to slay the dragons in the caves."

"Maybe, or maybe she just puts the teeth in her collection."

"Or she just gives the teeth to mermaids to enter Atlantis."
"What do the mermaids use the teeth for?"

"To help keep Atlantis a secret. They use the teeth under water to look like rocks."

"Maybe she just likes to keep the teeth because they are shiny and strong."

"Or they are so shiny that she uses them to find her way through the enchanted forest where she keeps her home."

"Maybe she just likes visiting kids and giving them all of her money."

"Or maybe there is more than one tooth fairy.
They all have competitions, for who collected
the most teeth for that part of the world.
And they win a trophy...
or a bigger castle!"

Location of Teeth		Top Fairy	World Teeth Count
United States	1	Scarlett J.	...counting...
China	2	David L.	...counting...
North America	3	Jensen D.	...counting...
South America	4	Quincy T.	...counting...
Europe	5	Lillian J.	...counting...

"Or maybe I just kept the tooth."

"No dad, that's silly!"

ABOUT THE AUTHOR

Julia Johnson is an author and illustrator that
enjoys getting to create children's books for her
own three children as well as others. She most
enjoys creating literature that helps children spark
their own imagination and wonder.